STAR WARS™

THE ADVENTURES OF BB-8

Written by David Fentiman

Written and Edited by David Fentiman
Project Art Editor Owen Bennett
Senior Designer David McDonald
Slipcase Designer Stefan Georgiou
Pre-Production Producer Kavita Varma
Senior Producer Alex Bell
Managing Editor Sadie Smith
Managing Art Editor Ron Stobbart
Creative Manager Sarah Harland
Art Director Lisa Lanzarini
Publisher Julie Ferris
Publishing Director Simon Beecroft

For Lucasfilm
Editorial Assistant Samantha Holland
Executive Editor Jonathan W. Rinzler
Image Archives Stacey Leong
Art Director Troy Alders
Story Group Leland Chee, Pablo Hidalgo and Rayne Roberts

This edition published in 2016.
First published in Great Britain in 2016
by Dorling Kindersley Limited
80 Strand, London, WC2R 0RL
A Penguin Random House Company

Slipcase UI: 001-305129-Oct/16

Page design copyright © 2016 Dorling Kindersley Limited.
A Penguin Random House Company

© and TM 2016 LUCASFILM LTD.

A CIP catalogue record for this book
is available from the British Library

ISBN 978-0-2412-0789-5

Printed and bound in China

www.dk.com
www.starwars.com

A WORLD OF IDEAS:
SEE ALL THERE IS TO KNOW

Contents

BB-8

The galaxy is full of droids. There are big ones, small ones, helpful ones and dangerous ones.

One of these droids is called BB-8. BB-8 is an astromech droid. Astromechs help starpilots fly their ships through space.

BB-8 belongs to Poe Dameron. Poe is the bravest pilot in the Resistance. The Resistance is a group that protects the galaxy from the evil First Order.

The First Order

The First Order wants to conquer the galaxy. Poe and the other members of the Resistance must stop it. The Resistance is led by General Leia.

Many years ago, Leia and her brother, Luke Skywalker, defeated the evil Galactic Empire.
The members of the Empire who escaped became the First Order.
Now the First Order wants revenge!

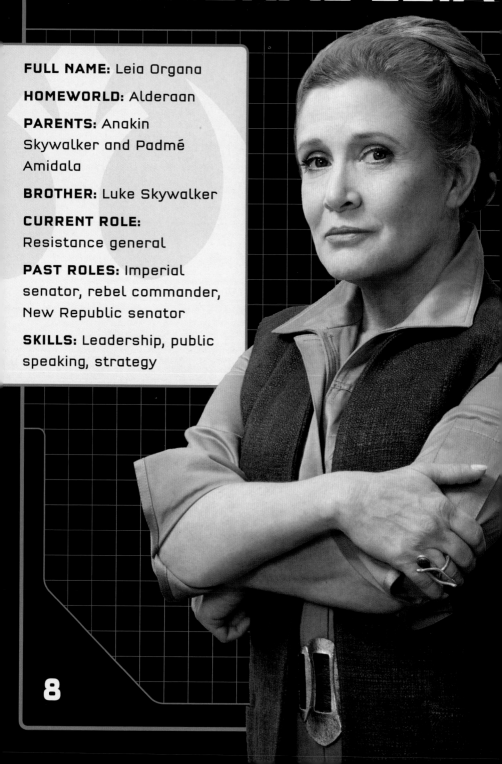

›GENERAL LEIA

FULL NAME: Leia Organa

HOMEWORLD: Alderaan

PARENTS: Anakin Skywalker and Padmé Amidala

BROTHER: Luke Skywalker

CURRENT ROLE: Resistance general

PAST ROLES: Imperial senator, rebel commander, New Republic senator

SKILLS: Leadership, public speaking, strategy

General Leia at the Resistance base

PROFILE:

- Leia fought bravely in the war against the Empire.

- She has now formed a new group to defend the galaxy from the First Order. This group is known as the Resistance.

- Leia's brother, Luke Skywalker, disappeared many years ago. Leia is trying to find him. She hopes that Luke will help her.

The village

BB-8 and Poe fly to the planet
Jakku to meet a man called
Lor San Tekka. Lor is an
explorer who has a map that
the Resistance needs. The map
shows where Luke Skywalker is.

Lor gives Poe the map, but then the First Order attacks Lor's village and takes Poe prisoner. Just before he is captured, Poe gives the map to BB-8. The brave little droid escapes into the desert.

In the desert

After Poe gets captured, BB-8 is left on his own. He is stuck in Jakku's hot desert, with no idea which way to go.

All BB-8 can do is roll towards the horizon, and hope to find someone who will help him.

BB-8 does not realise that he is being watched. A hungry creature called a nightwatcher worm is following him. Luckily, droids aren't very tasty, and it leaves him alone.

Meeting Rey

BB-8 is rolling through the
desert, trying to find help.
Suddenly he gets caught in
a net. A grouchy scavenger
called Teedo has grabbed him!

Teedo likes to take droids
apart to steal their technology.
Another scavenger called Rey
hears BB-8's frightened beeping,
and she rushes over to rescue him.
Rey agrees to take BB-8 to a
town called Niima Outpost.

Welcome To
NIIMA OUTPOST

Niima can be a confusing place, so here is a guide for new arrivals.

Unkar Plutt

RULE NUMBER 1

Get scavenging. You will have to go into the Starship Graveyard and bring back technology to trade.

RULE NUMBER 2

Carry a blaster. Jakku is dangerous, with lots of hungry monsters and gangs of thieves. You will need to protect yourself.

RULE NUMBER 3

No fighting! Constable Zuvio will arrest anyone who makes trouble.

RULE NUMBER 4

Don't upset Unkar Plutt. Unkar is Niima's biggest, meanest junk boss. He has a gang of thugs that he sends after people who make him angry.

Constable Zuvio

Escape!

At Niima Outpost, BB-8 and
Rey are chased by First Order
stormtroopers. They run into
an ex-stormtrooper called Finn.
He is also being chased by
the First Order.

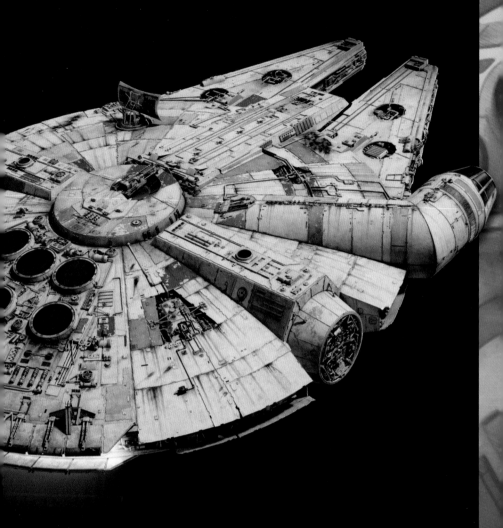

Together, BB-8, Rey and Finn
steal an old starship called the
Millennium Falcon, and escape
from Jakku. They get attacked by
First Order ships, but Finn shoots
the enemy down!

Han and Chewbacca

Just when Rey and Finn think they are safe, the *Millennium Falcon* breaks down! They are left floating helpless in space.

While Rey and Finn try to fix it, an enormous cargo ship appears. It swallows the *Millennium Falcon* whole!

The cargo ship belongs to Han Solo and Chewbacca. They are two legendary smugglers who used to own the *Millennium Falcon.*

Gangsters

BB-8 is nervous about Han and
Chewie, but it turns out they
are friendly. They are very happy
to have their old ship back.

Suddenly some gangsters board Han's cargo ship. They are enemies of Han and Chewie! The scary Guavians wear red, and the scruffy Kanjiklub wear black.

There is a big battle, but BB-8 and his friends manage to escape on the *Millennium Falcon*. Han takes a look at the map BB-8 is carrying. Half of it is missing!

Maz's castle

Han and Chewie think that
they should get some help.
They take BB-8, Finn and
Rey to visit an old friend of
theirs called Maz. Maz is a
pirate who lives in a castle.

Maz's castle is very old.
It stands next to a lake on the
planet Takodana. The castle
is full of pirates and smugglers.
BB-8 has never seen so many
aliens in one place before.

BATTLE AT MAZ'S!

Rey and BB-8 are exploring Maz's castle. Rey finds herself being drawn towards the castle's dark basement.

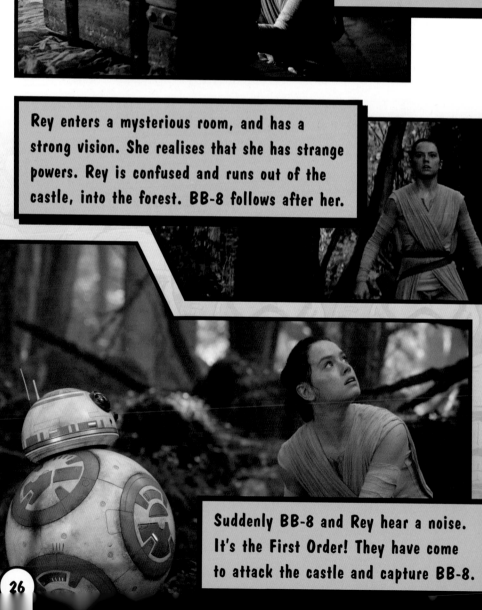

Rey enters a mysterious room, and has a strong vision. She realises that she has strange powers. Rey is confused and runs out of the castle, into the forest. BB-8 follows after her.

Suddenly BB-8 and Rey hear a noise. It's the First Order! They have come to attack the castle and capture BB-8.

The castle has been destroyed, and stormtroopers are everywhere. Finn, Han and Chewie try to fight back.

The Resistance has arrived! Its X-wings battle the First Order's TIE fighters.

Kylo Ren is the First Order's greatest warrior. He wears a mask and carries a lightsaber. Kylo attacks Rey in the forest and takes her prisoner.

The First Order retreats, and General Leia arrives in a transport. She meets with Han, Finn, Chewie and BB-8. They realise that Rey has been captured.

Battle plan

After the battle at Maz's castle, BB-8 and his friends travel to the Resistance base on the planet D'Qar.

Rey has been captured, and the First Order has revealed its powerful secret weapon. It is known as the Starkiller.

The Starkiller can destroy an entire star system. With this weapon, the First Order will be able to conquer the galaxy!

The Resistance has to destroy the Starkiller. The Resistance pilots put together a daring plan to attack it.

PILOT'S LOG:
JESS PAVA

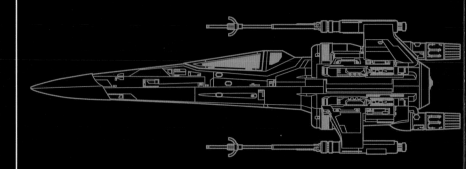

🔴 Blue and Red squadrons are going to attack the Starkiller. I'm not nervous. Our X-wings are faster and stronger than the First Order's TIE fighters.

✪ My code name will be Blue Three. Commander Poe is going to lead us, and he always brings us victory.

✪ BB-8 has come back to the Resistance base. I'm glad to see him. I thought he had been destroyed.

✪ I should get some sleep. It's going to be a big day tomorrow!

Reunited with Poe

BB-8 hasn't seen Poe Dameron since Poe was captured on Jakku. The Resistance must have rescued him, and BB-8 is very happy to see Poe again.

BB-8 will fly in Poe's X-wing for the attack on the Starkiller.

BB-8 has been in many battles before, so he is not scared.

Poe is going to fly a special black and orange X-wing, called *Black One*. This is BB-8's favourite ship.

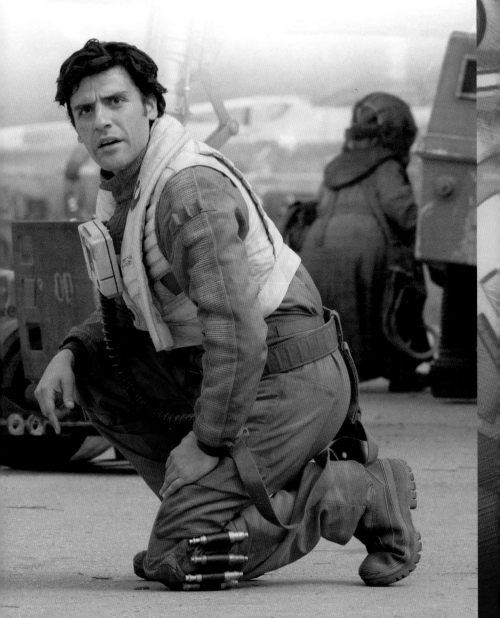

C-3PO and R2-D2

At the Resistance base,
BB-8 meets two very
famous droids,
C-3PO and R2-D2.
They both once
belonged to
Luke Skywalker,
General Leia's
brother.

C-3PO and R2-D2
helped Luke and
Leia defeat the
evil Empire.

After the war, Luke disappeared and R2-D2 went silent. R2 has been shut down ever since.

C-3PO serves Leia as her assistant. He always talks to R2 even though R2 never talks back!

BB-8's friends

There are many droids serving with BB-8 in the Resistance. They each do different jobs, but they are all important.

NAME: PZ-4CO
CLASS: Communications droid (translates messages)

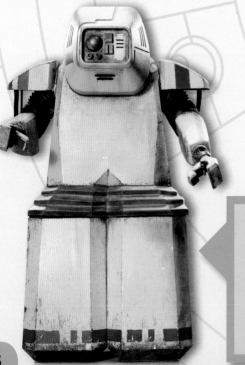

NAME: B-U4D
CLASS: Loading droid (maintains X-wing fighters)

NAME: M9-G8
CLASS: Astromech droid (helps starship pilots)

NAME: GA-97
CLASS: Spy droid (keeps watch for the First Order)

NAME: 4B-EG-6
CLASS: Power droid (a big walking battery)

Attacking the Starkiller

The Resistance pilots fly to attack the Starkiller. BB-8 joins Poe in his special X-wing starfighter.

Rey manages to escape from her cell, and she meets up with Han, Chewie and Finn. They attack the Starkiller on the ground, while Poe and his pilots battle the First Order's TIE fighters.

BB-8 is very brave. After a hard battle, the Resistance finally manages to destroy the Starkiller.

Poe and BB-8 fly back to the
Resistance base. BB-8 is happy
to still be in one piece!

Victory!

Back at the Resistance base, everyone is happy that the Starkiller has been destroyed. It was a tough battle, and some of the Resistance did not return. Finn was wounded, but Rey rescued him.

R2-D2 wakes up, and realises that he has the missing half of BB-8's map. They put the map back together. Now they know where Luke is! Rey is going to find him. Everyone watches as she takes off in the *Millennium Falcon*.

Quiz

1. What kind of droid is BB-8?

2. Who does BB-8 belong to?

3. Who does Rey rescue BB-8 from?

4. What planet is Maz's castle on?

5. What is the name of
   Poe's special X-wing?

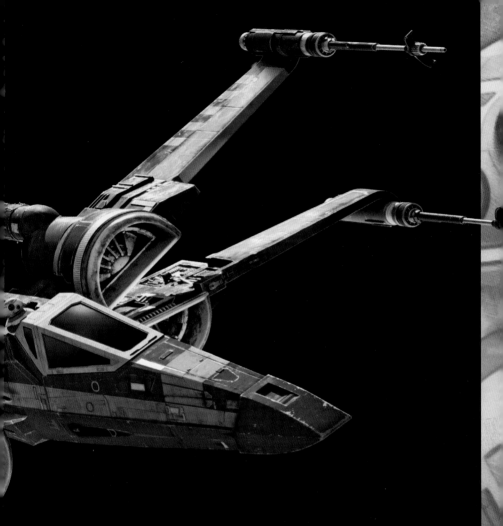

6. What is the First Order's secret weapon?

7. What is Jess Pava's code name?

8. Which droid serves as Leia's assistant?

9. Who has the missing half of BB-8's map?

Answers on page 47

Glossary

Blaster
A weapon that fires glowing bolts of energy

Conquer
To take control of something using force

Droid
A robot

Empire
An evil group that once ruled the galaxy, but which was destroyed

Explorer
Someone who travels to places that no one has been to before

First Order
A new army formed by the survivors of the Empire

Leadership
The ability to lead people well

Mysterious
Strange, or hard to explain

Nervous
To feel worried or scared

Resistance
A group created to protect the galaxy from the First Order

Retreat
To escape from a battle or situation

Reunited
When things that were once together, but then separated, are put back together again

Scavenger
Someone who searches through worthless junk to find useful things

Senator
A member of a senate (a type of government)

Smuggler
Someone who transports illegal goods

Starkiller
A giant secret weapon built on an icy planet by the First Order

Technology
Equipment made using scientific knowledge

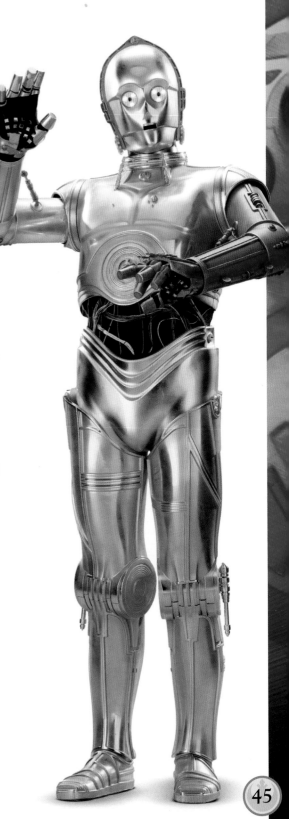

Index

Answers to the quiz on pages 42 and 43:
1. astromech droid 2. Poe Dameron 3. Teedo 4. Takodana
5. *Black One* 6. the Starkiller 7. Blue 3 8. C-3PO 9. R2-D2

A Note to Parents

DK READERS is a compelling programme for beginning readers, designed in conjunction with leading literacy experts, including Maureen Fernandes, B.Ed (Hons). Maureen has spent many years teaching literacy, both in the classroom and as a consultant in schools.

Beautiful illustrations and superb full-colour photographs combine with engaging, easy-to-read stories to offer a fresh approach to each subject in the series. Each DK READER is guaranteed to capture a child's interest while developing his or her reading skills, general knowledge, and love of reading.

The five levels of DK READERS are aimed at different reading abilities, enabling you to choose the books that are exactly right for your child:

Pre-level 1: Learning to read
Level 1: Beginning to read
Level 2: Beginning to read alone
Level 3: Reading alone
Level 4: Proficient readers

The "normal" age at which a child begins to read can be anywhere from three to eight years old. Adult participation through the lower levels is very helpful for providing encouragement, discussing storylines, and sounding out unfamiliar words.

No matter which level you select, you can be sure that you are helping your child learn to read, then read to learn!